This edition published by Parragon Books Ltd in 2014 and distributed by

Parragon Inc.
440 Park Avenue South, 13th Floor
New York, NY 10016
www.parragon.com

ISBN 978-1-4723-6725-9

Printed in China

Oliver Twist

Based on the original
story by Charles Dickens

Illustrated by
Sophie Burrows

PaRragon

Bath • New York • Cologne • Melbourne • Delhi
Hong Kong • Shenzhen • Singapore • Amsterdam

Oliver Twist was born in the workhouse. His mother pressed her cold, white lips against his forehead, fell back—and died.

Oliver found his place at once: an orphan, to be tossed about and beaten through the world, despised by all and pitied by none.

Since there was no one to look after him in the workhouse, Oliver was sent to live with the elderly Mrs. Mann. She kept most of the money she was given to feed the children in her care for herself, and many of them died. By Oliver's ninth birthday, he was a pale, thin child. But he had a good, sturdy spirit.

One day, Mr. Bumble, the beadle in charge of the workhouse said, "Oliver Twist is too old to remain here. We have decided to take him back to the workhouse. Will you come along with me, Oliver?"

Mrs. Mann gave Oliver a thousand embraces and (what Oliver wanted a lot more) a piece of bread and butter—in case he seemed hungry when he got to the workhouse, and it looked as if she wasn't taking good care of the children.

As Oliver was led away from the wretched home where he had never had one kind word or look, he burst into an agony of childish grief. His loneliness sank into his heart for the first time. That night, Oliver sobbed himself to sleep on a rough, hard, workhouse bed.

The boys in the workhouse were fed in a large stone hall, with a cauldron at one end. From this, the master ladled gruel, a thin mix of oats and water. Each boy had one small bowl and no more. The bowls never needed washing; the boys polished them with their spoons till they shone again.

Finally, the boys were so wild with hunger they decided someone should ask for more. The task fell to Oliver Twist.

The evening arrived. The gruel was served and disappeared; the boys whispered and winked at Oliver. He was desperate with hunger. Advancing to the master, bowl in hand, he said:

"Please, sir, I want some more."

The master turned very pale.

"What?" he boomed.

"Please, sir," repeated Oliver, "I want some more."

The master hit Oliver on the head with the ladle and shrieked for the beadle.

Next morning, a notice was pasted on the gate offering a small sum of money to anybody who would take Oliver Twist to be an apprentice to any trade. It was arranged that he should go to Mr. Sowerberry, the undertaker.

"Dear me!" said the undertaker's wife when Oliver arrived. "He's very small."

Charlotte, the maid, led Oliver downstairs and gave Oliver a plateful of coarse, broken scraps of food the dog had left. Oliver tore the bits apart hungrily, eating them quickly.

"Your bed's under the shop counter," said Mrs. Sowerberry. "You don't mind sleeping among the coffins, I suppose?"

Oliver gazed around him with dread. An unfinished coffin stood in the middle of the shop, and the space for his mattress looked like a grave.

Mr. Sowerberry had an assistant, Noah Claypole. Noah bullied Oliver. One day, he pulled Oliver's hair and said, "How's your mother?"

"She's dead," replied Oliver.

"Yer mother was a regular bad 'un. And it's better that she died when she did, or else she'd have been hung."

Oliver seized Noah by the throat and shook him till his teeth chattered.

"Charlotte! Missis!" blubbered Noah.

Charlotte and Mrs. Sowerberry dragged Oliver, struggling and shouting, into the cellar and locked him up for the rest of the day. When he was put back among the coffins for the night, he wept for a long time. Then he tied the little clothing he had into a bundle and, at first light, stepped into the street.

A milestone showed that it was seventy miles to London. "London!" thought Oliver. Nobody would ever find him there! He walked until his feet were sore and his legs so weak that they trembled. Early on the seventh morning, he limped into the little town of Barnet. He sat on a doorstep, covered with dust and with bleeding feet.

Then one of the strangest-looking boys Oliver had ever seen came up to him. The boy was short, with bowed legs and a stubby nose, and he wore a huge man's coat with the cuffs turned back.

"Hullo, mate! What's going on with you?" he said to Oliver.

"I'm so hungry and tired," replied Oliver.

"I suppose you want somewhere to sleep tonight," said the strange boy. "Do you have any family?"

"No," said Oliver.

"Stick with me, then," said the boy.

Oliver discovered that his new friend's name was Jack Dawkins, but most people called him "the Artful Dodger."

When they arrived in London, the Dodger took Oliver to a grim-looking house. The walls and ceiling were black with age and dirt, and Oliver felt anxious, thinking he shouldn't have come. A very old man, with matted red hair, stood frying sausages. Four boys were seated around a table. They grinned at Oliver.

"Fagin," said the Dodger, "this is my friend, Oliver Twist."

The man grinned.

"We're very glad to see you, Oliver," he said, offering him a plate of food.

After breakfast the next day, Fagin, the Dodger, and another boy, Charley Bates, played what Oliver thought was a curious game. Fagin trotted up and down the room with a walking stick. The two boys followed him closely and pinched items from him as he walked. If he felt a hand in any of his pockets, Fagin cried out where the hand was, and then the game began all over again.

After a while, the Dodger and Charley went out with two young ladies named Bet and Nancy.

"Is my handkerchief hanging out of my pocket, my dear?" said Fagin to Oliver, when they had gone. "See if you can take it out without my feeling it, as you saw them do this morning."

"Here it is, sir," said Oliver, showing it in his hand.

"You're a clever boy, my dear," said Fagin, patting Oliver on the head.

After many days, Oliver begged Fagin to allow him to go out with Charley and the Dodger. Fagin agreed, and the three boys set off. The Dodger made a sudden stop.

"Do you see that old guy at the bookstall?" he asked. Charley nodded.

The two boys crept close behind the old gentleman.

To Oliver's horror, the Dodger plunged his hand into the gentleman's pocket and drew out a handkerchief! Then the Dodger and Charley ran away at full speed. Oliver made off as fast as he could, too. The old gentleman hurried after him, shouting, "Stop, thief!" A crowd followed, and at last, Oliver was stopped. A police officer seized him by the collar and dragged him along the streets to the magistrate.

The robbed gentleman, Mr. Brownlow, explained he had chased Oliver just because he had seen him running away. But he was a kindly gentleman, and if it was not Oliver who had robbed him—and he couldn't be sure—he didn't want to get him into trouble.

Just then, Oliver fainted.

"He has been hurt!" Mr. Brownlow said. "I fear that he is ill."

An elderly man rushed into the office.

"Wait!" he cried. "The robbery was committed by another boy. I saw it."

Worried about Oliver's health, Mr. Brownlow called a coach and took Oliver to his own house in Pentonville.

For many days, Oliver lay sick in bed. But at last, he was well enough to sit up with the housekeeper, Mrs. Bedwin, eating bits of toast broken into broth. He had only been there a few minutes when Mr. Brownlow walked in.

"Poor boy!" he said. "How do you feel, my dear?"

"Very happy, sir," replied Oliver. "And very grateful indeed, sir."

"Why! Mrs. Bedwin, look!" said the old gentleman.

He pointed to a picture of a woman on the wall and then to Oliver's face. Every feature was the same. Mr. Brownlow turned to Oliver. Now that he saw the resemblance to someone once dear to him, he was determined to help the boy.

The days of Oliver's recovery were happy ones. Mr. Brownlow provided new clothes for him, and Oliver gave his old clothes to a servant to sell.

One day, Mr. Brownlow had some books to return to a bookseller. Oliver was eager to be helpful, so Mr. Brownlow sent him with the books and some money to pay the bookseller.

"He'll join his old thieving friends and laugh at you," said Mr. Grimwig, a friend who was visiting Mr. Brownlow. "If that boy ever returns to this house, I'll eat my head."

But Mr. Brownlow trusted that Oliver would return.

As Oliver Twist was walking along, he felt a pair of arms thrown tightly around his neck.

"Don't!" cried Oliver, struggling. "Let go of me!"

"Oh, goodness!" said Nancy. "I've found him! Oh! Oliver!"

"Young Oliver!" cried a man. It was Bill Sikes, another of Fagin's gang. "Come home directly!"

"That's not my home!" cried Oliver, struggling. "Help!"

But no help was near. In another moment, Oliver was dragged into a maze of dark, narrow streets.

"Delighted to see you looking so well, my dear," said Fagin when they got to the house. Sikes took the money from Oliver, and the others took his books and his new clothes off him.

"Oh, pray send back the books and money," begged Oliver. "He'll think I stole them!"

"You're right," remarked Fagin. "He *will* think you have stolen 'em. Ha!"

At first, Oliver was kept locked in a room alone, but after a week he was allowed to wander around the house. He noticed again how dirty it was, how different from Mr. Brownlow's. And he felt desperate at losing the kind affection he had enjoyed there.

"Why don't you work for Fagin?" said Charley.

"I don't like it," said Oliver timidly. "I—I—would rather go."

From that day, Oliver was seldom left alone and was always with the two boys, who played the old game with Fagin every day.

One night, Nancy took Oliver to help Bill Sikes. Bill and Oliver walked for more than a day and a night and eventually came to a house surrounded by a high wall, which they climbed. Oliver realized that they were going to break in.

He sank to his knees. "Oh, let me go!" he cried. "Do not make me steal!"

But Sikes took no notice. He put Oliver through a little window at the back of the house.

"Go along the hall to the door and let me in," whispered Sikes.

Oliver decided to dart upstairs and alert the family.

"Come back!" cried Sikes fiercely.

Scared, Oliver dropped his lantern. Two men appeared at the top of the stairs. Oliver turned to run, but fell down the stairs and hit his head hard on the wooden steps. He staggered back and out of the door.

"How the boy bleeds!" Sikes said. He dragged Oliver by the collar into a field, then left him lying in a ditch and ran. A cold, deadly feeling crept over Oliver's heart, and he saw and heard no more. He lay motionless in the ditch.

Finally, Oliver awoke and staggered to a road. He saw a house and made toward it. As he drew nearer, he saw it was the house they had attempted to rob. He knocked at the door, then collapsed.

The door opened.

"A boy!" exclaimed one of the men from the night before. He dragged Oliver into the hall, calling, "Here's one of the thieves, wounded!"

"Is the poor creature much hurt?" whispered a female voice. She sent for the doctor, Mr. Losberne.

As well as the bump on his head, Oliver had a fever. He was ill for many weeks, but he eventually grew better under the care of the doctor and the ladies of the house, Mrs. Maylie and Rose.

"Mr. Brownlow would be pleased to know how happy I am," said Oliver one day. So Mr. Losberne took him in a carriage to visit Mr. Brownlow. But alas! The house was empty. The servant next door told them that Mr. Brownlow had gone away.

When the warm weather came, Mrs. Maylie, Rose, and Oliver went to stay at a cottage in the country. One day, Mrs. Maylie sent Oliver to a nearby town with a letter. On his way home, Oliver stumbled against a man in a cloak.

"Ha!" cried the man. "Rot you! I could have got rid of you ages ago! What are you doing here?"

His words meant nothing to Oliver, who gazed in amazement at the madman (for such he supposed he must be) and then returned home.

A few days later, Oliver fell asleep at his window and dreamt, in terror, that he was in Fagin's house. Fagin was there, with another man in a large cloak.

"Hush!" Fagin said. "It's him, sure enough."

"Him!" the other man answered. "If you buried him fifty feet deep and took me across his grave, I should know that he lay buried there."

Oliver awoke. At the window, peering into the room, stood Fagin! And beside him, white with rage, was the strange man he'd bumped into. In an instant, they were gone.

Oliver called for help. Everyone hunted in the yard and fields, but in vain.

Meanwhile, back in Oliver's hometown, Mr. Bumble had married the woman in charge of the children and staff in the workhouse.

"Are you going to sit there snoring all day?" asked Mrs. Bumble one evening. "Be off!"

So Mr. Bumble went to a tavern, where he noticed a man in a large cloak staring at him.

"I've seen you before," said the man. "I want some information from you." He pushed a couple of gold coins across the table. "Think back twelve years. A boy was born in the workhouse ..."

"Young Oliver Twist!" said Mr. Bumble.

"Yes, I spotted him the other day. Where is the hag that nursed his mother?"

"She died last winter," said Mr. Bumble. But he was cunning. Wanting more gold, he told the stranger that his wife knew more. They arranged to meet next day.

"What name am I to ask for?" said Mr. Bumble.

"Monks," replied the man, and he strode away.

Mr. and Mrs. Bumble went the next day to meet Monks in an old building by the river.

"You were with this hag the night she died?" Monks asked Mrs. Bumble. "And she told you something ..."

"About Oliver's mother," she replied. "Yes. Give me the gold, and I'll tell you all I know."

Monks handed over the gold coins.

"The nurse and I were alone when she died," Mrs. Bumble began. "She said she had stolen gold from Oliver's dead mother. After the nurse died, I found a scrap of dirty paper in her hand—a pawnbroker's ticket. I took it and collected the item."

Mrs. Bumble threw a small bag on the table. Monks tore it open, taking out a little gold locket holding two curls of hair and a plain gold wedding ring.

"It has 'Agnes' engraved on the inside," said Mrs. Bumble.

Monks tugged an iron ring in the floor, pulling up a large trapdoor. Water was rushing rapidly below. He dropped the items into the stream, and they were gone.

"Now get out," he said to the Bumbles. "Go on, go!"

The next evening, Nancy overheard Fagin and Monks talking about a lady named Rose who was staying in a hotel in London with Oliver and Mr. Losberne. Nancy had a good heart and truly wanted Oliver to have a better life than hers. She hurried to the hotel in the morning and asked to see Rose. It was her only chance to help the young lad, and she would take it if she could.

"I'm about to put my life in your hands," Nancy said. "I am the girl that dragged little Oliver back to Fagin's on the night he left the house in Pentonville."

"You!" said Rose.

"I, lady!" replied the girl. "Do you know a man named Monks?"

"No," said Rose.

"He knows you," Nancy replied, "and he knew you were here—I overheard him say so. Monks saw Oliver accidentally on the day we first lost him at the bookstall. He realized Oliver was the child he had been watching for, though I don't know why. He struck a bargain with Fagin that, if he got Oliver back, Fagin would pay. Last night, I heard Monks say, 'The only proofs of the boy's identity lie at the bottom of the river.' Then he said, 'Fagin, you never made such traps as I'll set for my young brother Oliver.'"

"His brother!" exclaimed Rose.

"Those were his words," said Nancy.

"What should I do? How can I help Oliver?" said Rose. "Where can I find you again if I need you?"

"Every Sunday night, from eleven until twelve," said Nancy, "I will walk on London Bridge, if I am alive."

The next day, Oliver, who had been out walking, rushed into the room where Rose sat.

"I have seen Mr. Brownlow," he said, "getting out of a coach and going into a house."

"Quickly!" she said. "I will take you there directly."

When they arrived, Rose left Oliver in the coach and went in alone. She was presented to two elderly gentlemen.

"Mr. Brownlow, I believe, sir?" said Rose.

"That is my name," said one old gentleman. "This is my friend, Mr. Grimwig."

"I shall surprise you very much," said Rose, "but you once showed great goodness to a dear young friend of mine: Oliver Twist."

Rose explained everything that had happened to Oliver since he left Mr. Brownlow's house.

"Thank God!" said the old gentleman. "This is a great happiness to me. But where is he now?"

"He is waiting outside," replied Rose.

She hurried out of the room and returned, accompanied by Oliver.

"There is somebody else who should not be forgotten," said Mr. Brownlow. "Send Mrs. Bedwin here."

"It is my little boy!" cried the housekeeper, embracing him.

After a happy visit, Rose and Oliver returned home.

The following Sunday night, as the church bell struck eleven, Nancy put on her bonnet.

"Wait!" cried Sikes. "Where's the gal going to at this time of night?"

"I'm not feeling well," said Nancy. "I want a breath of air."

"You won't have it," replied Sikes, suspicious. He rose, locked the door to their home, and took the key.

"Let me go—this minute!" cried Nancy.

"No!" said Sikes. He dragged her, struggling, into a small room, where he held her down by force. She struggled until twelve o'clock had struck, and then gave up.

Soon after, at Fagin's house, Fagin said to one of his gang, Bolter, "I want you to follow a woman. Tell me where Nancy goes, who she sees, what she says."

The next Sunday night, Bill allowed Nancy to leave, and Bolter followed her.
She went to the center of a bridge, where she stopped. Rose, accompanied by
Mr. Brownlow, arrived in a carriage, and Nancy went toward them.

"Not here," Nancy said. "Come down these steps!"

Mr. Brownlow told Nancy that she must point out Fagin to him.

"I will not!" cried the girl. "I will never do it. He has been good to me!"

"Then," said Mr. Brownlow, "I want Monks."

Nancy explained when and where to find Monks, and
described him. "He is tall, strongly made; he has a lurching walk;
his eyes are sunk deep in his head; upon his throat, there is …"

"A red mark, like a burn?" cried Mr. Brownlow.

"You know him!" said Nancy.

"I think I do," he said.

When they left the bridge, Bolter crept back to Fagin's house and told him all that he had seen and heard.

Later, before daybreak, Fagin sat watching the door as Bolter slept. When Sikes turned up, Fagin hauled Bolter out of bed.

"Tell me again about Nancy, just for him to hear," said Fagin, pointing to Sikes. "How you followed her, and a gentleman and lady asked her to give up all her pals, and Monks first, which she did—and to describe him, which she did—and to tell her where we meet."

"Hell's fire!" cried Sikes. He dashed home and roused Nancy from her sleep.

"Bill," said the girl, "why do you look at me like that! Tell me what I have done!"

"You know, you she-devil!" answered Sikes. "You were watched tonight; every word was heard."

"Then spare me!" Nancy cried. "I refused to betray you and Fagin! So spare me!" But Sikes was too angry to listen. He hit her, and she staggered, fell, and hit her head. She had time to breathe one last prayer before she died.

When the sun lit up the room where the dead woman lay, Sikes fled.

That same day, Mr. Brownlow found Monks, where Nancy said he would be, and had him brought to his house.

"Because I was your father's friend," he said, "I will treat you gently now."

"What do you want with me?" said Monks.

"You have a brother, as I believe you know," said Mr. Brownlow. "After your father separated from your mother, he fell in love with someone else— Oliver's mother, Agnes. He died before they could marry. I have a portrait of the poor girl." He gestured to the painting on the wall. "When Oliver crossed my path, and I rescued him from a life of vice—"

"What?" cried Monks.

"—and he lay recovering in my house, I saw how much he looked like her portrait. He was snatched away before I found out his history. I thought you might know where to find him and tried to trace you, but until two hours ago, I hadn't managed to find you.

"You destroyed the proof of Oliver's birth so that he should not inherit any of your father's money. There was a locket that would have shown us who Oliver's mother was, and you got it from Mrs. Bumble and dropped it into the river. I've figured you out, Monks."

While Monks was at Mr. Brownlow's house, a group of Fagin's robbers were sitting in the upper room of a ruined house.

"When was Fagin took?" one said.

"At dinner time. And the Dodger has been took, too."

There came hurried knocking at the door below. It was Sikes.

"Tonight's paper says Fagin's took by the police. Is it true?" Sikes asked.

"True."

"And—it—Nancy's body—was found?" Sikes asked.
The group nodded.

"It should be buried!" he shouted. "Now, who's that?"

Outside, an angry crowd was gathering. The story of the murder had gotten out, and everyone knew Sikes must have killed Nancy. The public had come to get him. Sikes opened the window and shouted, "Do your worst! I'll cheat you yet!"

"Give me a rope, a long rope," he cried to one of the robbers. He climbed out of the house and onto the rooftop, planning his escape. But when the crowd roared upon seeing him, he lost his footing, slipped, and fell. That was the last of Bill Sikes.

Two days later, Oliver met with Mrs. Maylie, Rose, Mr. Brownlow, and the man Oliver had seen looking in at the window with Fagin.

Monks cast a look of hate at the astonished boy.

"This child," announced Mr. Brownlow, "is Monks's half-brother, the son of his father, by Agnes Fleming, who died giving birth in the workhouse. Tell Oliver, Monks."

Scowling at the trembling boy, the greedy Monks told the whole story again of how he had helped to destroy the documents that left Oliver a share of his father's money, and dropped the locket and ring into the river so that no one should know who Oliver was.

At last, Mr. Brownlow turned to Rose.

"Give me your hand," he said gently. "Agnes had a sister, and that sister is Rose. You are Oliver's aunt." Turning to the others, he explained, "Their father died, and Rose lived in poverty until Mrs. Maylie saw the girl, pitied her, and took her home."

The little that remains of Oliver's story can be told in a few words.

The court was packed for Fagin's trial, but not a rustle was heard as the verdict was announced: guilty.

Monks retired to America, where he had a chance to start a new life— but, once more, he fell into his old ways and ended his life in prison.

Mr. and Mrs. Bumble had their jobs taken from them and ended up in the very same workhouse that they had once run.

Rose married happily, and Mrs. Maylie moved to live with Rose and her new husband.

And Mr. Brownlow adopted Oliver as his son, giving Oliver a life as near to one of perfect happiness as can ever be known in this changing world.